Shadowland

Chapter One

"You're always busy," Cecilia complained. "Working, working, family, some secret project, being alone, working, alone..."

"I get it," Brennan said dryly. "I'm not a social butterfly lately. Things chnage, Cil. I'm more focused on my job and being a good aunt and sister, and taking time for myself. It's very theraputic." She walked down the hall to the kitchen, balancing the phone on her ear as she ran a brush through her shoulder-length honey-brown hair.

"Theraputic my ass. I think you're hiding out, ever since the imploding relationship that got you out of Derek-ville for good."

Brennan sighed, grabbing an apple and yogurt from the fridge. "I am not hiding out. I'm a busy person. I love all of you guys but I'm not available every time you call. Life's more than partying."

"So that's a definite no to the concert in Hartford this afternoon?"

"A definite no," Brennan confirmed, scooping all the mail that had piled up over the past month off her kitchen table. As she did so, a silver-and-white wedding invitation caught her eye. She pulled it out of the pile, running her finger over the engraved, elaborate script. "I'm actually not working today but I have plans. Very important ones I can't break."

"Fine. But you only have yourself to blame when you completely fall off everyone's social radar and we all think you died."

Shaking her head, Brennan grabbed her purse, leaving the invitation on the counter. Glancing at it one last time she walked out of the apartment, locking the door behind her.

Parking her car behind the familiar silver Camry, Brennan walked up to the front door, letting herself in.

Gabe was sitting in front of the TV wtching one of those Japanese cartoons Brennan couldn't stand, devouring a stack of pancakes drenched in syrup, oblivious to the fact that someone just entered his house.

"Someone could come in and rob you blind, take the clothes off your back, and you wouldn't even notice," Brennan told him. She st next to him on the couch, helping herself to a bite of his pancakes. "God this stuff is horrible," she muttered as she glanced at the TV screen. "Haven't I been a little bit better of an influence on you?"

"You just can't appreciate good television," Gabe replied.

"You don't know what good television is," she countered. "Are you ready to go yet?"

Gabe finished his last bite. "Now I am."

"Here." Brennan handed him a large box wrapped in newspaper. "Happy birthday."

Gabe accepted it, raising an eyebrow.

"I didn't have any wrapping paper," she told him with a shrug.

Gabe tore into the paper eagerly, obviously curious. His expectant expression turned into utter joy and amazement when he revealed his gift. "You got me Guitar Hero!"

"Your mom won't approve, say you spend too much time in a technologically-induced state as it is but personally I think it's because she can't work anything more sophisticated than a toaster. Besides, at least this way I know you're experiencing good music instead of the crap you're exposed to now."

Gabe threw his arms around her. "Did I ever tell you you're my favorite aunt?"

"I'm your only aunt," Brennan reminded him. "But I can still be your favorite. You only turn ten once...so enjoy it. Now get dressed. We have a full day ahead."

Brennan went into the kitchen while she waited, seeing balloons tied to one of the chairs and an elaborately decorated cake on the counter. Her phone began to ring, breaking into the quiet. "Hello?"

"Hey Bren," Krista's voice came over the line. "You there yet?"

"Just now. Already gave him his gift."

Krista sighed. "You got it, didn't you?"

"Of course I did. The kid's drowning in crappy entertainment. I needed to save him while I still could."

"So he can be a head-banging beer-guzzler like his aunt?"

"I do not *guzzle* beer," Brennan said in a mock offended tone. "I down it. There's a difference. It wouldn't kill you, you know, to access your inner party rocker chick sometimes. I remember all the concerts, the tattoo that got you grounded for a millenium—"

"That was a long time ago. I'd say we've both grown up since then."

Brennan sighed. "Tht's what I hear. According to Cecilia I've pretty much died socially."

"Farbeit from me to agree with Cecilia but maybe she's got a point. There's more to life than work."

"Says the woman who has a meeting on her son's birthday."

"I know. I'm not going to be winning Parent of the Year any time soon. It's bad enough I have to work but Wes too-"

"That's why you're lucky your favorite sister is an editor with flexible hours."

"I really appreciate this, Bren. Wes and I have been so busy lately and now..."

"It's all taken care of," Brennan assured her. "We've got plenty to do today. It'll be a hell of a birthday, I promise." She heard footsteps pounding down the stairs. "He's ready so we're going. Want to talk to him?"

"I've already called him three times. I think he needs a break." Krista paused. "You're not upset you couldn't make it to the wedding are you?"

Brennan had wondered who would bring it up first. "I'm not sure I would've gone anyway. I mean, I love the Jensens and we've stayed in touch but I haven't seen Will since I was seventeen. Awkward."

"Maybe. But I still think you should see him while he's in town. You only have one high school sweetheart, Bren, and it's obvious you've never gotten over-"

"Ready to go, Aunt Bren?"

Brennan looked up to see Gabe standing eagerly in front of her. She nodded, putting her arm around him as they headed for the door. "We're on our way," she told her sister. "See you tonight." She hung up the phone and turned to Gabe. "Your mom says hi."

"Again?" Gabe rolled his eyes.

"I'm sure it won't be the last time today either."

As they left the house Brennan thought about what Krista had started to say before Gabe came downstairs. Then she shook the thought from her mind and turned her attention to Gabe. This day was about her nephew, not shadows from the past.

Chapter Two

Brennan drove into town, heading to the city zoo. "You're sure this is where you want to go first?"

"Are you kidding? All of these killing machines in one place? Who wouldn't?"

This time Brennan rolled her eyes.

She let Gabe lead her around, stopping everywhere he wanted. She snapped a few pictures of him outside the hyena, snake, and bear cages with her phone, sending them to Krista's and Wes's phones. After they'd seen everything she took Gabe to an annual spring carnival across the town square, taking more pictures of him on rides and trying to knock down the bottles with his "wicked curve ball".

They went to the concession stand and got corn dogs and cotton candy, both of which Gabe insisted was mandantory, and began walking down Main Street. "The movie theater isn't far and it's a nice day so we're walking," Brennan told Gabe. "I've got to have some way to work off all of our lovely food choices here." She took a big bite of her corndog.

"Did you get a lot of good pictures?" Gabe wanted to know between bitefuls.

Brennan nodded. "The video of us on the rollercoaster too. I already sent it all to your parents. Want to see?"

Gabe nodded and they stopped walking on the sidewalk. They threw away the remains of their food and Brennan took out her phone, playing the video.

The picture jerked and shook as the ride moved and twisted around, catching Gabe's and Brennan's shrieks and yells. Gabe looked up at her. "I'm really having fun today," he told her. "I always have fun with you."

Brennan felt her heart melt. "Right back at you. It doesn't bother you that I'm around all the time does it? Popping in a couple times a week, Sunday family dinners...don't want to give you too much family togetherness." She winked.

Gabe shook his head. "I like it. You're a cool aunt."

"Thanks." She bent down and looked at him seriously. "I know it doesn't make up for your not having grandparents-on our side anyway-but you'll always have us. No matter what."

Gabe had been asking a lot of questions about his grandparents lately. Krista said he was getting to that ag, where he wanted to know where he came from. It was hard on Krista and Brennan, who rarely spoke of their parents, of that painful time. But Gabe had a right to know and Krista broke down and finally told him the truth.

Gabe nodded. "I know."

As Brennan straightened up she saw she had a missed call. They resumed walking as she checked who it was from. *Beth Jensen?* she thought with a frown. *Why is she calling me while her son is getting married?*

"Aunt Brennan, what's going on?" Gabe asked suddenly.

Brennan looked up to see a man running down the street, coming from the bank. He looked panicked and terrified; shouts came from behind him and Brennan could see he was being chased by three armed police officers.

Wrapping her arm protectively around Gabe, Brennan cautiously backed up. When she saw them heading their way, she grabbed Gabe and prepared to take him into the store behind them.

Before she could react there were screams: the man had pulled a gun while the police officers attempted to apprehend him, a wild look in his eye that reminded Brennan of the caged animals they saw earlier.

Then she heard it: the loud, unmistakable sound of a gunshot. As if it happened in slow motion, Brennan could see the man being tackled as a stray shot escaped from his gun. The gun haphazardly pointed in hers' and Gabe's direction.

Without hesitation she dove in front of her nephew as the ctivity around her began to blur, the sounds turning into a dull roar, as if it were all happening from far off.

Then she felt it.

It started off as a dull sting, then intensified into a burning, firey sensation that ripped apart her insides, causing her pain she'd never before experienced. She was vaguely aware that she was no longer in front of Gabe but on the hard, concrete sidewalk, surrounded by blurry, disconnected images of strangers swirling around her, moving their lips but she was unable to discern what was coming from them. She managed to look upward and saw Gabe staring down at her, frightened and frozen with shock.

Frightened but alive.

Grateful for that knowledge, she felt her body begin to relax, felt the burning pain convert into creeping numbness that slowly began to claim her body. She looked up at Gabe again, taking in the bright splatters of blood on his T-shirt. Her blood.

"Gabe," she croaked, looking at his terrified face. She focused on it as everything else began to fade. "Love you...little man. Tell...your mom..." She couldn't hold on any longer.

Feeling the remaining strength leave her body, Brennan felt herself let go.

Chapter Three

Feeling heavily drugged from sleep, Brennan slowly opened her eyes.

Her bedroom was dark, the shades drawn just as she left them. Rolling over on her bed, Brennan groggily looked at the bright red numbers on her alarm clock, glowing brilliantly in the darkness.

5:45 a.m.

Frowning, Brennan slowly sat up, realizing she'd slept on top of the covers, in her clothes. She slid off the bed and walked out of her room, down the hall into the den. As she looked around the room she couldn't shake the feeling that something wasn't right. Yet she had no idea what it was.

She slowly sank onto the couch, trying to decipher the nagging feeling she couldn't ignore. Something was wrong...

She felt as though she'd slept a hundred years. Everything felt so vague, so disconnected. For the life of her, she couldn't remember what happened the day before or even what day it was. Much less why she slept in her clothes and was awake before six a.m.

Do I have a meeting today? she wondered. *We're supposed to go over—*She stopped, frowning. *That's weird. I can't remember what book I'm working on.* She shook her head. *Maybe I've been partying too hard. Cecilia wanted to go to a concert; maybe I'm wasted. That would explain why everything's a blur.*

She slowly stood and walked past the wall where a framed portrait of her, Krista, Wes, and Gabe hung and stopped. Staring at the photograph she knew so well, she felt the nagging sensation return, only much sharper than before. Something about Gabe...

Of course! Today was Gabe's birthday. *I've got to get going. I have to pick his gift up, find out if the* carnival's today, check movie times... She ran toward the door.

Suddenly, she wasn't where she'd been. Instead of her apartment she was in the middle of town, a few yards away from Main Street. *What the hell?* she wondered, confused. *How can I be here when I was just at my apartment?* Then it hit her, the one thing that made sense.

She was dreaming.

That explanation suited her just fine. Feeling lighter now that the burden of confusion had lifted, Brennan let out her breath slowly to relax and then decided to stroll down Main Street.

She felt compelled to head in a certain direction; her feet seemed to have a mind of their own, leading her down the sidewalk without her knowing where she was headed or why.

She finally came to a stop at Charlie's Mini-Mart, across the square from the bank. An unsettling feeling washed over her, covering her body in chills.

Then she saw it: someone was removing the yellow caution tape that had roped off a small area in front of the store. In the middle of it was a dark, disturbing stain.

Brennan frowned. Something was frantically pulling at the corners of her mind, something about this particular spot...

A sound exploded in her mind, as loud and vivid as though it'd actually happened. *That's because it has,* she realized in alarm. *Gunfire. Right here on this sidewalk. That dark stain...it's blood. Someone was hit.*

She froze in horror. *Not someone...Gabe.*

Before she even realized it, she was running. This was no dream. It didn't occur to her to call her sister or to get to her car...the only thing she was focused on was getting to the hospital.

Because she was so focused she made it there in record time. *Anglehearst General. It has to be this one...* She ran up behind a couple as they stepped in front of the automatic doors and followed them inside.

Brennan looked around wildly, unsure of where to go. The nurses' station was swamped with people and Brennan couldn't wait. A sense of urgency was more than overwhelming.

She went into the elevator with a large group of people, forgetting her normal discomfort with crowded elevators. She got off at the next floor with a harried-looking young couple, figuring she could try this nurses' station.

As it turned out, she didn't have to bother. A few yards down the hall, kneeling in front of someone sitting in a chair outside the I.C.U., was the unmistakable dark-blonde hair of her sister.

Brennan broke into a run, seeing Wes pace the length of the hall while talking on the phone, a worried expression on his face. Brennan felt her insides wrench, knowing it had to be Gabe in the I.C.U.

She reached out to touch her sister's shoulder then stopped abruptly. Krista's body shifted slightly, revealing the person she was talking to in the chair.

Gabe.

Relief flooded Brennan as she looked him over; he appeared to be fine. "Thank God you're okay," she said. "I was so scared..." She trailed off, something catchng her eye.

The TV in the waiting room across from the I.C.U. was on, tuned in to a newscast. Brennan walked a few steps forward, listening to the reporter.

"...the shooting on April 4th, one week ago today," the woman was saying, sitting in the studio and obviously reading from the teleprompter.

April fourth? Brennan thought in confusion. *Today's April fourth, Gabe's birthday. We were on Main Street and someone shot at us...* She slowly turned back to where her family waited. *Who's in the I.C.U.?* she thought suddenly. *Why is that reporter saying it's April eleventh?*

Why didn't Gabe or Krista look at me when I talked to them?

An uncontrollable foreboding feeling began to rise in her chest, swelling and expanding like a balloon. She walked·past her sister and nephew to the door, which was partway opened. She had to see who was inside.

She cautiously approached the bed, not having the courage to look at the person's face. Something prevented her from doing so, something she couldn't explain. Instead, she stared at the foot of the bed for what seemed an eternity, until she could take the suspense no longer.

Her eyes began to travel upward, taking in a woman's still form tucked in with thick hospital blankets. Her arms were free, resting on top of the covers, firmly against her body. Her knuckles were scraped raw and her arms were covered in scratches.

Instinctively, Brennan looked down at her own hands and arms, running her fingers over the smooth skin. Only it shouldn't have been because she could vaguely remember the sting she felt when her knuckles and arms scraped the concrete as she fell. Fell while jumping in front of something...

She looked back at the still woman, at the honey-brown hair resting on top of the pillow, at the nose, the mouth, and face she knew so well: she'd seen them all in the mirror every day for twenty-seven years.

Feeling her insides lurch uncontrollably, she took in all the tubes and wires connecting the woman to the machines that kept her alive. But it wasn't just any woman.

As hard and inexplicable as it was to digest...the woman Brennan was staring at wasn't a reflection in the mirror or a window. Somehow, some way Brennan was staring at herself, lying unmoving in a hospital bed.

"This is impossible," Brennan murmured. "I'm walking, I'm talking, I feel fine..." She looked down at her yellow T-shirt which was completely free of the dark blood the hd soaked it earlier. It was more than possible. Though it made no sense, it was completely real.

Brennan collapsed to the floor in shock and disbelief.

Chapter Four

Brennan sat on the floor staring up in a daze at her body laying in the bed, trying to control her breathing, which was on the verge of hyperventilation. Her heart was pounding in her ears so strongly it felt more like drums, and her pulse was racing faster than she could ever remember it racing before.

That she could feel any of this was incredibly ironic.

More like insane, she thought, hugging her knees to her chest. *A spirit can't "feel" anything.*

Is that what I am now? A spirit?

Brennan had never believed in the paranormal: ghosts, hauntings, out-of-body experiences...they were just urban legends. But now...this changed everything.

Brennan looked up as nurse entered the room and began to check her vitals. "There's no point of me asking if you can hear me or not, is there?" she asked.

The nurse continued to work with her back turned, completely oblivious.

"Worth a shot," Brennan muttered.

More footsteps nearby caught her attention. Looking out the window, Brennan could see a doctor talking to Krista and Wes. Scrambling to her feet, Brennan ran out of the room before the nurse closed the door.

"It's been a week," Krista was saying, her face etched with worry. "You said if she didn't wake up in a few days that would mean she's in a coma. Is that what you're telling me now? My sister's in a coma?"

The word *coma* hit Brennan like a bucket of ice, chilling her to the bone.

"Yes, Mrs. Norton, that's what I'm telling you," the doctor replied gravely. "Your sister lost a lot of blood and sustained serious damage to her heart—"

"How?" Wes wanted to know. "She was shot in the stomach."

"She went into cardiac arrest," the doctor reminded him. "She died on the table when she was brought in. We managed to rescusitate her but the damage to her heart was already done."

I died? Brennan thought in disbelief. *Is that why I'm like this? My spirit left my body and it can't get back in because I'm in a coma?* Even thinking it Brennan felt ridiculous but in some, strange way it made sense.

"Why won't she wake up?" Krista was asking. "Has her brain been affected too?"

"Brennan's suffered a trauma," he explained. "It's affected several organs in her body that control basic functions. A coma is the body's way of shutting down to repair itself. Brennan sustained a head injury when she hit the ground but my concern right now is her heart."

"Will my sister wake up, Dr. Landers?" Krista asked quietly.

"I don't know," Dr. Landers answered honsetly. "We're doing everything we can for your sister."

Brennan watched the doctor walk away, unexplainable anger rising in her chest. "That's it?" she yelled after him. "You drop a bomb like that on my sister and you don't offer a solution? Why won't you help us? What kind of doctor are you?" She stopped her tirade with effort and looked back at her family.

Gabe was asleep in the chair and Krista was sobbing into Wes's chest while he held her tightly, trying to comfort her. Brennan felt like someone was ripping her guts out as she watched; seeing the pain they were in was unbearable.

Brennan couldn't stand it anymore. Seeing herself in a hospital bed, learning her heart stopped and now she was in a coma, seeing her normally tough, collected older sister who she thought was indestructble fall apart before her very eyes and not being able to comfort her...it was too much to handle.

Brennan broke into a run, desperate to get away from it all, feeling like she was suffocating. Before she even realized it she was on the highway, running toward the bridge.

She stopped, grabbing onto the railing and screaming with all her might, with everything she had in her. *We lost our parents,* Brennan thought bitterly. *Now Krista might lose me...she doesn't deserve this! Our family's been through enough! She doesn't deserve to lose her sister.*

I don't deserve to die.

The anguish overwhelming her, Brennan continued to scream and cry out in earnest, the pain in her chest slicing like a knife. *I'm young, I have a great career, a wonderful family, good friends, plans for the future...this can't be it. This can't be it.*

As her cries subsided Brennan looked over the railing to the water far below. Without thinking about it she climbed onto the railing, carefully stepping over it. She knew it wouldn't do any good, knew it wouldn't fix anything...but she didn't care. *It's not like I can get hurt like this anyway*, she thought bitterly.

Taking a deep breath, she prepared to jump in the water below.

Then she felt the last thing she expected to feel. She had to be hallucinating. *A hallucinating spirit*, she thought, close to hysteria. *That's rich.* But how else could she explain the hand, calm and reassuring, that she suddenly felt on her shoulder?

"It's okay, Bren," a soft voice close to her ear spoke. "You're not alone."

Brennan felt her entire body go rigid. She knew that voice, knew it as well as she knew her own.

Whirling around she looked directly into the clear blue eyes, the kindest eyes she'd ever known. The sandy blonde hair, the familiar expression...

She was looking into the fce of Will Jensen. And he could touch her, see her...

Without warning, she threw her arms around him, never so happy to see anyone in her life.

Chapter Five

They embraced for a long time, just standing there holding one another, not wanting to let go of the only thing they could really feel. When they finally broke apart they stared at each other in amazement. "Will," Brennan breathed. "You can see me, we can touch...how?" Then it hit her. "Something happened to you too, didn't it?"

Will nodded. "I'm in bad shape." He looked out over the bridge. "I thought about jumping too...but what's the point?"

"We don't get a say in anything anymore," Brennan said bitterly. She shook her head. "What's happening to us?"

"Best I can figure it...your spirit has to go somewhere," Will told her. "We're not dead but we're barely alive so we're somewhere in between. Wandering around aimlessly and no one's the wiser."

"This is insane. All of it. It has be some kind of nightmare..."

Will held out his hand to her. "Come with me."

They ended back up at Anglehearst General, passing the second, third, fourth, and fifth floors. When they arrived on the sixth, Will led Brennan down the hall.

Stewart and Beth Jensen were pacing in front of the room, whispering and low, anxious tones. Will's brother Brad and his fiancee Stacey were sitting in the same comfortable chairs Brennan recognized from the second floor, Stacey's head resting against Brad's shoulder.

Will led her to the window where they could get a good look inside. Brennan's breath caught in her throat s she saw Will inside, hooked up to monitors just like she was. Thick white bandages were wrapped around the top of his head, his neck was in a brace, and a breathing tube was placed down his throat.

Brennan turned to him next to her in horror. "What happened to you?" she whispered.

"I don't remember much," he admitted, "but from what I overheard from my family and the doctor I was in a car accident the night before Brad's wedding. Lost control, drove off the bridge...I guess that's why I can't stay away from there."

"I'm sorry," Brennan told him, shocked.

Will looked back at Brad and Stacey. "They should be married right now," he said softly. "Instead they're spending what should have been their honeymoon in the hospital."

"I know," Brennan said softly. "It was Gabe's birthday when I..." She trailed off, looking confused.

Will led her away from his family and they sat in the waiting room. "What do you remember?" he asked gently.

Brennan frowned, concentrating. "Gabe and I were on Main Street, on our way to the movies. Then we saw a man being chased by the cops, coming right toward us. I grabbed Gabe and was about to run when I heard...an explosion. I could feel myself fall...the last thing I remember was looking up at Gabe. Then I woke up in my bedroom and it was a week later."

"It was kind of like that for me. I remember driving on the bridge, in a hurry I think, then...I think I lost control. I remember water...the next thing I know I'm sitting across from the church where the wedding was supposed to be on a park bench. Two days had passed. I've been hanging out at the hospital and the bridge ever since...and then I saw you."

"Why weren't you surprised to see me?" Brennan asked suspicisously.

"I haven't had a lot to do," he said ruefully, shrugging. "I started wandering around the hospital...and i couldn't believe it when I saw you in the I.C.U." His voice was thick with emotion. "It broke my heart seeing you like that."

"Did you look for me?" Brennan asked quietly, remembering feeling the same way when she saw him like that just moments ago.

"I tried but I couldn't find you. I was starting to think it was just me, that I was losing it. Then I saw you on the bridge."

Brennan smiled wryly. "Is it sick to feel relieved to not be the only spirit wandering around?"

Will chuckled. "Then we're both sick then."

Brennan immediately sobered. "It's been on the news, hasn't it? What happened to me."

Will nodded, wincing slightly at the memory.

"Tell me," she urged. "Fill in the blank spots."

He hesitated. "Brennan-"

"Please."

He sighed. "His name is Andrew Scott. He tried to rob the bank but an employee tripped the silent alarm. When the cops came he was already running down the street, panicked. When they tried to arrest him he freaked out and his gun accidentally went off." He paused. "Witnesses say the shot headed toward a child and the woman he was with threw herself in the way just in time." He looked at her in admiration.

"It's fuzzy," Brennan told him. "I don't remember thinking about anything, I just remember falling." She paused. "I'm so grateful he's okay."

Will looked at her in disbelief. "Brennan-"

"Do you hear that?" Brennan interrupted. "Over the PA."

Will strained his ears to listen. "Paging Dr. Landers," a nurse's voice requested urgently. "Dr. Landers to the second floor I.C.U."

Will locked eyes with Brennan. "That's you," he said in alarm.

They rced to the second floor, just in time to see the nurses and Dr. Landers working frantically in Brennan's room. Wes and Krista stood outside, clinging to one another in silent horror.

Brennan raced to the window , watching the blur of activity while some kind of alarm was going off. The scene was unimaginable; it made her sick to her stomach.

Then she fell to the floor, dizziness overcoming her. Will grabbed her shoulder and began calling her name in alarm but Brennan was scarcely aware of it. She felt like her insides were being ripped out; she also felt an overwhelming pulling sensation, so strong...

Suddenly, she realized what it meant. *It's pulling me away from here. Pulling me toward death.*

But not if I stop it.

She let out a long breath, gasping for air. As she struggling to breathe she was dimly aware that the alarm in the backyard had ceased.

"Brennan?"

She looked up into Will's anxious eyes, at the concern etched into his expression. "I'm okay," she managed, letting him pull her to a standing posistion. Then she stared into the I.C.U.

Her monitors were beeping normally again; she appeared to be out of immediate danger. Dr. Landers came out into the hall, approaching Krista and Wes.

"Her heartrate dropped," Dr. Landers explained. "She was close to flat-lining again."

"Is she okay now?" Krista demanded.

"She's stable, for now. But her heart..." He trailed off. "The most important thing is to make sure it doesn't stop again. The trauma caused by her injuries has put her heart under enormous strain."

"What can we do?" Wes wanted to know.

"Wait." After a moment's hesitation, he disappeared down the hall.

Brennan stood by Will in shock. It was too unbelievably to be real. All of it.

Will patted her on the shoulder and was about to say something when Krista let out a cry of frustration, causing Brennan to jump slightly.

"Krista-" Wes began, trying to touch her reasurringly.

She shook him off, beginning to pace rapidly. "Wait? All we can is wait? Is that supposed to help?"

"Krista, you're in a hospital. You've got to calm down-"

She whirled on him. "I don't care! That's my sister in there, my baby sister-" She broke off, dissolving into sobs.

As Wes attempted to comfort her, Brennan began to back away. "I can't stand here and watch this. This is Krista, my indesctructable, superpowered older sister-" She stopped when she saw Krista break away from Wes and go into the I.C.U.

"Go," Will told her. "Maybe it'll help."

Brennan watched her sister pull achair up next to her bed and sit down. Looking back at Will one last time, Brennan went into the room.

Trying to overcome the unsettling feeling she got from seeing herself in a hospital bed, Brennan instead focused on her sister, who gently picked up her hand. Brennan looked down at her hands, hoping for a sensation, but there wasn't one.

"You know I've never cared much for doctors," Krista began, "so I'm certainly not going to listen to one now. I don't care what he says-" She broke off, her voice faltering. Then she took a deep breath to collect herself, forcing a small smile. "Gabe thinks you're a hero," she said, wiping her eyes with her free hand. "He's been telling everyone he knows about his supercool, heroic aunt." She paused. "You are, you know. You saved my little boy, Bren, and I can't begin to express how grateful I am for that. But I'm selfish. I want more. I can't lose you. We've...we've both already lost enough, wouldn't you say?" She shook her hed. "You were just a kid," she said softly. "You were Gabe's age when they died...it must've been so hard for you. I was a senior, getting ready for graduation, preparing for college...and both our lives got turned upsidedown. I was devastated; I didn't have a clue what to do, how to go on...but then I saw you, this sweet, innocent, once carefree kid who no longer had parents and I knew, right then, what I had to do. I had to put my own grief aside because you needed me." She smiled wryly. "There were times I wanted to strangle you, times I wanted to run screaming down the street...you were the most stubborn, strong-willed person I ever met. I can see so much of you in Gabe sometimes when he's mouthing off, testing my patience...but also when he's pouring over a book or playing air guitar with the stereo or eating a whole mushroom and pepper pizza in one sitting. He's got your talent for listening, too, and one of the most generous hearts I've ever seen. Like his aunt's." She squeezed Brennan's hand. "I want you to know that I've never regretted my decision to raise you, to become your legal guardian. I felt like you deserved more than an eighteen-year-old could give at times but I knew no one else on the planet would love you as much and be able to remind you, everyday of where you came from. You didn't have to be uprooted from everything you knew...and you had someone who understood." She let out a shaky breath. "I know you've felt guilty over the years, like you were a burden, but I'm telling you right now that could never be true. Raising you was a priveledge, Bren, not a chore. You grew up to be an amazing woman...and thanks to you, my son will grow up to be an amazing man." Her voice cracked. "And I hate to ask you for more after what you've done...but I have to ask you to fight. You have a family who needs you and we won't let you go. Feel that. Feel us. Let it be enough to keep you going." She stood and leaned over, kissing Brennan on the forehead. "I won't leave this hospital until you let me know I need to."

Brennan watched her sister leave the room and tears streamed down her face. She'd never doubted her sister's love for her but to hear her pour her heart out like that...Brennan had never felt more valued and appreciated in her life.

She looked up to see Will waiting respectfully outside the room, leaning against the opposite wall. She looked up at him, nodding that it was okay for him to come inside.

Will took her hand and led her to a nearby chair. "That looked intense," he told her quietly. "Are you alright?"

"How can I be alright?" Brennan demanded, pulling her hand from his. "It's hard enough seeing myself lying motionless in a hospital bed, hooked up to tubes and wires–" She jerked her head toward the bed–"but then I have to watch my sister break down and plead for e to keep fighting. Even though I was right across from her, could reach out and try to touch her...she couldn't know it. She wasn't sure if I could hear her; but I can and every word..." Brennan trailed off, turning away. "She talked about raising me after Mom and Dad died, seventeen years ago next month. She talked about it being a priveledge and an honor, and how she sees so much of me in Gabe and how grateful she is for me saving his life...but she can't lose me. Not just because we lost our parents but because it's almost like I was her kid, too, in a way," Brennan realized. "She feels as maternal toward me as she does Gabe, though she'd never admit it to me because she'd be afraid I'd think she was trying to replace Mom. And she didn't...she just continued on. I teenage girl raising a ten-year-old and now she has her own. That's why she's Superwoman. That's why she can't handle–" Brennan broke off. Then she stood. "I'm sorry I bit your head off. You've been nothing but great to me–"

"It's okay," Will assured her. "Given the circumstances...you could call me every name in the book in any language you want. I'd say you've earned it."

"So have you," she reminded him.

"But I've had a little longer to process everything. You just are letting it all sink in. Cut yourself a break."

They sat in silence for a moment, both visibly uncomfortble by their location.

"Let's get out of here," Will said suddenly. "I think we've had enough of hospitls for the moment."

Brennan couldn't agree more. "Where do you want to go?"

"That's the beauty of it," he told her as they walked down the hall. "We could go anywhere we want."

"You're right," Brennan said, remembering. "If I think of a place, I instantly go there. It's like we're free to roam except..."

"...the pull we get to the last place we were when it happened," Will finished. "And the hospital."

"That's a good sign," Brennan said as they exited the building. "It means, in some small way, we're still connected to our bodies. Our lives."

Will didn't comment as he led the wy down the sidewalk but Brennan had to believe it was true.

The alternative was unbearable.

Chapter Six

"So," Will asked as they walked down the street. "Where do you want to go?"

"Anglehearst High School," she replied immediately without thinking.

Will looked surprised but agreed. "Okay. Anglehearst High it is."

Brennan closed her eyes and thought of her old high school, the towering three-story building, the lush green football field, and the stadium bleachers.

When she opened her eyes Brennan was sitting on the top bleacher seat, and she looked out over the field fondly. She'd never been one of those people who wished they were back in high school but something about being back there, looking at the field glowing under the sunlight, was reasurring. Safe.

"Kind of cool, huh?" Will's voice came suddenly from beside her.

Brennan jumped, startled. "You scared the crap out of me," she said, hitting him playfully on the arm. "It's creepy."

"But awesome."

"If we were on *Star Trek* maybe." Brennan continued to look around. ""Feels weird to be back here, doesn't it?"

"You know the reunion's coming up right?" Will asked. "Ten years since we've seen this place."

"We can make fun of all the jocks that got fat and lost their hair," she joked. "Or the cheerleaders with three kids at home." She sobered up quickly. "If we make it here."

Will placed a comforting hand on her shoulder. "Do you remember the night I asked you out?" he asked in an obvious attempt to redirect her thoughts.

Brennan could see it clearly in her mind. "I was in the parking lot with my friends, smoking cigarettes Amanda stole from her older brother. We were talking about my upcoming sixteenth birthday when a water balloon hit me in the back of the head," she finished wryly.

"I had to get your attention somehow," he said with a shrug. "If it makes you feel any better, I was aiming for your bag."

"Good thing you never tried out for baseball with an arm like that," she quipped. "Anyway your friends started throwing the balloons at my friends so we retaliated by pouring our bottles of Coke on you and chasing you around the parking lot."

"And we ended up alone by my car," Will continued, "wet and sticky, our hair and clothes plastered to our skin...and I thought you were beautiful," he finished simply. "So I asked you out."

"And I said–"

"–'only if I pick the time and place'," Will quoted. "'There's still too much I don't know about you, Will Jensen'."

"Wow," Brennan said, impressed. "You have a good memory."

"Details stick out sometimes," he said with a shrug. "Especially good ones."

They sat there for a moment, just taking in the atmosphere. Then Brennan turned to Will abruptly. "Why California?"

Will frowned. "What?"

"I get wanting to get out of here, and Berkeley's a great school, and that you loved it so much you stayed there. And things turned out well for you, having your own landscaping company...but why there and not somewhere around here?"

"You mean somewhere near here," he corrected. "Like Cloumbia with you."

Brennan blushed slightly. "It just ended," she told him quietly. "You waited until graduation, when I thought we were going out to celebrate, and you drop the bomb on me that you're moving across the country. And that was just it."

"I knew your plans, about going to Columbia," he told her. "I know you wanted out of this nowhere town and how much you always wanted to go to New York. And I could've went with you and we would've stayed together but you weren't happy, Bren. You did a great job of hiding it but you deserved more. More than I could give you then. So I thought a clean break was best."

"In other words, you decided for me." Brennan stood. "Didn't you think I had a say-so too? Didn't my input count?"

"Of course it did—"

Brennan shook her head. "This is absurd. We were kids. We're only talking about this because of where we are and the situation we're in."

"Maybe not." Will stood as well. "I missed you," he admitted. "I cme back for Brad's wedding, to see my family, but I wanted to see you too, see how you've been. As I understand you're quite a good editor."

Brennan raised an eyebrow.

"Mom told me," he explained. "You know how the family always felt about you."

Brennan nodded. "That's why I was invited to the wedding."

"Would you have gone?"

Brennan hesitted. "I don't know," she admitted.

An uncomfortable sillence followed and Will broke it by clearing his throat. "Maybe we should go back now, see how our families are doing."

Brennan nodded, following him down the bleachers. "For the record," she said, turning to him, "I was the happiest I'd ever been. And it scared me."

"Why?"

"Because I was afraid to really get close to someone," she blurted. "I didn't want to lose them—"

"—the way you lost your parents," Will finished, understanding at once. "Wow," he said softly after a moment, reaching out to touch her hair. Brennan could feel a sensation as he did so. "Ten years later and we finally figure it out."

Brennan nodded. "Feels kind of good, huh?"

"That it does."

Before they knew it they were back at Anglehearst General, stopping at the second floor for her. A nurse was exiting Brennan's room, speaking to Krista. *You need to go home,* she thought, looking at her tired, worn-down sister. *Get some sleep, take care of yourself.*

"You're saying there's improvement?" Krista was saying. "In her brain activity?"

"According to the monitors, it's been increasing," the nurse replied. "Ever since this morning."

"But she almost flat-lined."

"That's due to the damage of her heart. But her brain activity is strong."

Brennan looked at Will. "It's increasing," she repeated. "Does that mean I'll wake up? And why since this morning?"

Without answering, Will pulled Brennan to him and kissed her.

Completely taken off guard, Brennan found herself kissing him back. When they broke apart Brennan looked at him. "I felt that," she said in amazement. "I mean I *really* felt it. But why-"

"Look," the nurse said suddenly to Krista and Wes. "It's improving still."

"She might wake up," Krista said excitedly, hugging Wes. "My God, she scared the hell out of me for a while there."

"That's why," Will told Brennan. "When we touch, it increases your brain's activity."

"Maybe it's doing it for you too," she told him. "Let's go to the sixth floor and check."

Will hesitated. "I'd rather be slone with my family for a while," he said finally. "If that's okay."

"Of course." Brennan squeezed his hand. "We'll meet up later."

After Will had gone Brennan turned her attention back to her sister, who was still talking to the nurse. "Remember, her heart is still a great concern," the nurse reminded her. "She's still not out of the woods yet. But she's making progress."

The relief on her sister's face lifted Brennan's spirits. "She's going to pull through this," she said confidently. "I know she is."

Wes kissed his wife on top of the head. "Of course she is. This is Brennan we're talking about. They don't make them tougher." He paused. "I think we should go home."

"I'm not leaving her," Krista said adamantly.

"You need rest," he told her. "Let's get our son from my parents, go home and have a meal together, and rest."

"She'll be alone," Krista whispered.

"No she won't. I spoke to Beth Jensen earlier and she said they'd come down soon."

"I still can't believe it about Will," Krista said, shaking her head. "If Brennan knew..." She trailed off. "Let me tell her we'll be back soon and we'll go," she said reluctantly. "But I'm coming back first thing tomorrow morning."

"Deal."

Brennan watched from the window as Krista kissed her lovingly on the forehead, promising to be back soon and telling her to keep hanging in there, that she was doing great. Then Krista slowly left the room and Brennan grazed her hand as she walked past. Krista suddenly smiled. "I know you're still here," she whispered, closing her eyes. "And I'll never give up on you."

Brennan watched them head to the elevator, starting to finally feel hopeful.

Chapter Seven

Brennan started to walk down the main hall of the sixth floor to see Will and the Jensens when she suddnely thought of Cecilia, surprised not to have sooner. *I wonder how she's taking it—*

Suddenly she was stnding in the middle of Cecilia's living room in her friend's apartment, noticing at once that it appeared s though a tornado had passed through. Mail was strewn over the coffeetable and the couches, shoes littered the floor, and laundry was draped over the arm-chair in the corner. *Cecilia's the neatest person I know,* Brennan thought, continuing to be shocked. *This doesn't even look like her apartment—*

"I don't care," Cecilia snapped, suddenly, coming in from the hall, the phone wedged between her shoulder and her ear as she buttoned up a simple white collared shirt. "Yes I know this is business, Sandra, but I can't just–" She broke off. "Fine. I'll be there in half an hour." She turned off the phone and hurled it across the room, letting out a cry of frustration that caused Brennan to jump. Then she sank into the messy arm-chair, putting her head in her hands. "Bren," she said softly. "Why'd you have to go and be a hero?" She looked up at the counter in the kitchen, at the framed photo of her and Brennan a couple of years earlier at their friend's engagement party, striking Charlie's Angels poses. "Because you're you," she answered herself, rising from the chair and walking over to the counter, picking up the photo. "I know you have a sister but me...I didn't. Until I met you." She replaced the photo, shaking her head. "I should be visiting you but instead I have to go into work and act like everything's fine..." She slowly backed away. "The truth is, work's not the only reason I've been staying away," she admitted. "I just...I can't see you like that," she blurted. "Hooked up to tubes, laying so still, not knowing if you can hear me or not...maybe it makes me a rotten best friend but I'll come to the hopital when I hear you're awake. becuse I know you will wake up. I'm just...sorry."

Brennan walked up next to her and squeezed her hand. "It's okay," she whispered. "I couldn't have a better best friend than you."

Cecilia took a breath. "Time to pull it together," she muttered. "And on the way home, I'm picking up a kick-ass clutch for you. And don't worry, it won't be pink."

Brennan chuckled. "Thank God for that," she said. Then she sobered, feeling horrible for how her condition affected her best friend. "I'm the one who's sorry," she whispered. "Not for saving Gabe but for all the pain I've caused."

"Brennan," she heard suddenly.

Brennan blinked and she was on the bridge, a few feet away from Will. He was grabbing onto the rail with one hand and clutching his head with another, crying out in agony.

Brennan ran to him, kneeling in front of him. "I'm here," she told him, grasping his hand that was on the railing. "It'll pass. But you have to fight it."

Will continued to cry out so Brennan pulled him close, starting to sing what they dubbed "their song" in high school.

They rocked back and forth for a while until Will pulled back, the pain he was going through reflecting in his eyes. But he stopped crying out and looked at Brennan, grasping onto her hand. She squeezed it back tightly.

After a long moment Will's grip loosened and he hugged her tightly. "I'm sorry," he said into her shoulder. "It's never been that bad except-"

"It's okay," Brennan told him, holding him. "You must've had one hell of a head injury in that accident. I wonder why nothing else is hurting you."

Will pulled back quickly. "We should leave," he said quickly. "I don't want to be here anymore."

"Do you want to go back to your family?"

He shook his head. "I want to go to Fort Lauderdale."

Brennan gaped at him. "Fort Lauderdale?" she repeated. "Are you insane?"

Will shook his head. "Why not? We're free, Brennan. We can do anything, go anywhere—"

"I don't think we should be that far from our families," Brennan interrupted. "Or...us."

"You know we can get back here in a blink, literally. What do you say?" He held out his hand to her.

"Why Fort Lauderdale?"

"You don't remember?"

"The summer after our sophomore year," Brennan said with a smile as it came to her. "We ran off without telling anyone and spent a weekend there. Krista grounded me for the rest of the summer."

"My parents were pissed too. But it was worth it." he looked at her meaningfully.

"Our first time," she said quietly. "In that motel with the tiny pool."

"Cliche that it was...it couldn't have been more special. For me anyway," he added quickly.

"For me too," Brennan assured him. Then she took his hand. "Okay. Let's go to Fort Lauderdale."

Chapter Eight

They arrived just as the sun was setting, sitting side-by-side on the beach looking out at the waves.

"This whole thing's crazy," Brennan said softly. "I've never believed in anything out of the ordinary. Nothing supernatural or paranormal...no spirits or whatever, yet here we sit." She gestured back and forth between them. "Unless this is all just a crazy dream."

Will shook his head. "You said it felt real when I kissed you, and your monitors proved it. As crazy as it is...this is real. No one else can see or hear us but it's real."

"And even more unbelievable is it happened to us around the same time," Brennan mused, focusing on the intense reds and golds in the sky as the sun slowly disappeared below the horizon. "Reuniting us after ten years...like this."

"Maybe it was supposed to happen," he told her quietly, transferring his gaze to her.

"Like fate? You've never believed in that before."

"Maybe I do now."

"Why are we really here?" she asked suddenly. "What don't you want me to know?"

"What are you talking about?"

Brennan took a breath and focused on the minor things that didn't add up that she'd been ignoring before. "You've been so evasive about your condition, you don't want me to see your family, and you wanted to come all the way to Florida. You're hiding something from me," she accused.

Will didn't meet her eyes. "Since when did you become so suspicious?"

"I'm not. It's just I used to be able to read you like a book, to tell when you were holding something back."

Will stood. "That was a long time ago." He paused. "Maybe we shouldn't have come here."

Brennan stood as well. "Maybe we shouldn't have," she agreed, starting to walk down the beach.

Will grabbed her by the arm. "Where are you going?" he demanded.

"Home," she replied. "To find out what you won't tell me."

"Bren-" He started but before he could finish she was gone.

Chapter Nine

Brennan dodged the nurses and the orderlies on the crowded sixth floor of Anglehearst General, heading for Will's room. She finally spotted the

Jensens-Will's parents and Brad and Stacey-outside Will's room speaking with a doctor.

"So that's why he had the accident," Stewart Jensen said slowly. "That's why he lost control of the car."

The doctor nodded. "Will's had this condition for sometime now. He never told any of you?"

Beth jensen shook her head, obviously still in shock. "Not a word," she said softly, burying her face in her husband's shoulder.

"I can't believe this," Brad said after the doctor had left. "Who the hell does he think he is, keeping a secret like that from his family?"

"Brad-" Mr. Jensen began.

"No!" Brad yelled angrily. Stacey touched his arm. "No," he repeated, lowering his voice. "What kind of person finds out they have a brain aneurysm waiting to happen and doesn't tell his parents? or his brother?" His voice cracked.

"Brain aneurysm?" Brennan echoed in confusion.

"Three months," a voice said from down the hall. "I've known for three months and I've never told a soul."

Brennan turned and saw Will sitting on the floor at the opposite end of the hallway, staring blankly ahead. Wordlessly, Brennan sat down across from him.

"I didn't want anyone to know I was dying." Brennan flinched at the word but he continued. "So I planned to come out here for the wedding, see my family and friends one more time. And you." He let out a long sigh. "The reason I didn't want you to come back to my room is because I found out earlier I'm braindead."

"Braindead?" Brennan whsipered, her insides clenching.

Will nodded. "That's why all the touching in the world won't help me." He looked at her. "The doctors in Bakersfield me it could rupture at any time, and one of three things would happen: I could be permnently paralyzed, lapse into a coma, or...die. When I was in that car that night it ruptured. I blacked out, obviously lost control of the car, and crashed off the bridge. Even if my brain was okay my body sure as hell isn't." He shook his head.

Brennan didn't know what to say at first. She wanted to be angry with him like Brad but how could she? It was his life; he had the right to choose what he did and didn't tell her. And after his revelation she could feel no anger. Only pain, shock, and a terrible, aching loss. "Where were you going?" she asked finally. "What was so important that you risked your life driving a car on the bridge when-"

"I was on my way to see you," he said simply.

"What?" she asked, her face draining of color.

Will nodded. "In case you didn't come to the wedding I wanted to see you...while I still could."

Brennan could hear what he wasn't saying: he'd expected this trip to be his last. "I'm the reason," she whispered. "I'm the reason you had the accident-"

"No," he interrupted firmly. "The aneurysm would've erupted no matter where I was or what I was doing. It was my choice to come and see you, though I'd had migraines all day. None of this is on you, Bren. None," he repeated, placing his hand on her shoulders.

She nodded. "I guess i can accept that. I still don't understand why you didn't tell anybody though."

"What good would it have done? I'd had second and third opinions and all pronoses were the same. There was nothing anyone could have done...so why waste the time making everyone sad and depressed when we could all be together, live like nothing changed...isn't that better?"

"I can understand that," she told him. "But I don't think your parents or Brad ever will."

He looked up at the ceiling. "I don't think that's going to matter much longer," he told her quietly.

"Will Jensen if you talk about giving up-"

"I'm not giving up," he told her. "I'm being realistic. I'm braindead, Brennan. I've made peace with it." He paused. "I'm not going to wake up."

"I might not either," she reminded him.

"No," he said suddenly, turning to her. "You still have a chance. What happened to you wasn't supposed to: you're young, healthy, with a long life ahead of you. You have people who love and depend on you. You're here because you took a bullet, a random act. I'm here because it's my time. An aneurysm is no 'accident'."

Brennan was about to argue whe she sudeenly lurched forward, clasping her hands to her chest. "My heart," she managed as Will watched, horrified.

Instantly they were in the I.C.U., while doctors and nurses worked to revive Brennan, who was flat-lining. "This is it," she gasped, doubled over in pain. "And I'm alone. Wes and Krista—"

Will wrapped his arms around her. "You're not alone," he told her. "I'm here and I'm not ready to let you go yet. Fight, Bren. Your family needs you. You're the glue that holds them together."

Brennan could see her hands blinking in and out and she knew she was fading. "I love them," she croaked. "And I—"

"I still love you, Brennan Fox. Stay with me."

Brennan held onto those words and managed topull herself back. Soon the room was in focus again, her chest no longer feeling like it was about to explode, and she could hear the monitors beeping normally again.

As she struggled to catch her breath she slowly looked up at Will. "You still love me?" she managed. "After all these years?"

He nodded. "Leaving you was the hardest thing I'd ever done. I thought I was doing the right thing but as time went by and relationships came and went I realized how much I regretted. You were my first love. And, as it turns out, the love of my life."

Brennan was speechless. "We were only kids," she whispered finally. "But I guess it doesn't really matter because you were my first love, too. And the reason none of my relationships never worked out was because no one was you. You had a part of me I couldn't give to them."

"So I guess that answers my question."

"Yes, I still love you too," Brennan said, kissing him. When she opened her eyes they were sitting at the park on a bench swing.

"Our favorite swing," she recalled. "How many times did we make out here?"

Will chuckled. "Too many to count." he put his arm around her as they looked up into the night sky, the moon shining down on them. "All we've been through...and here we are."

"It only took a brain aneurysm and a shootingto get us here," Brennan pointed out, snuggling against Will as he squeezed her gently, the swing swaying slightly in the breeze.

Chapter Ten

Brennan was surprised to wake up on the park swing, still in Will's arms. Then she felt alarmed. Who knew how much time could have passed...

"Will," she said urgently, shaking his shoulder. "Wake up."

His eyes opened and he smiled. "Morning beautiful," he said, kissing her on top of the head.

"Will," she said again. "We've been asleep."

Will's eyes widened as understanding dawned in them. "Which means it could be four months later for all we know."

"Evereything looks the same," Brennan observed as they got up from the swing. "So I don't think it's August."

"We need to get to a TV or a computer," he told her.

"My place," Brennan told him.

"But I don't know where—"

Brennan took his hand. "Come with me."

Seconds later they were in her living room. "Wow," Will commented, looking around. "You have a nice place."

"Thanks. The computer's back here." Brennan led him to her

spare room that she used as an office.

While Will looked around Brennan looked t her computer screen, which she'd luckily left on. "Two weeks?" she exclaimed.

"Two weeks?" Will echoed, coming up behind her. "Damn," he muttered.

"No more sleeping," Brennan ordered. "We've got to get to the hospital."

A moment later they were running through the second floor of the hospital, heading straight to Brennan's room.

It was empty.

Brennan just gaped at the empty bed. "Where am I?" she demanded. "I can't be dead...can I?"

"Not unless I am too," Will pointed out. "Come on. Let's find out what's going on."

She took his hand and he led her down the hallway to the nurses' station. "There's your chart," he told her, glancing at the pile of clipboards on the counter. "You've been moved to the sixth floor with me." His face darkened.

"What?" Brennan demanded. "What's so bad about being on the sixth floor?"

He looked t her carefully. "It's for people like me," he said finally. "People they don't expect to wake up because it's been three weeks."

Brennan stood there in shock. "They've given up on me?" she asked, her voice rising. "All the nruses and doctors in this damned hospital with their pricey equipment and their fancy degrees...and they've just given up?" she asked incredulously. "What happened in the past two weeks that made them write me off?"

"Let's find out," Will said, obviously perplexed. Within seconds they were on the sixth floor.

Brennan spotted Krista two halls over from Will's room and took off, hoping to get answers.

"I can't believe this," Krista was saying. "Three weeks ago we had hope and now they're telling me-"

"It's not over," Wes assured her. "She's on a donor list. There's still hope. She's the only person in the hospital who needs a heart transplant."

"Heart transplant?" Brennan repeated, looking at Will. "It's that bad?" She looked into her new room. "I really am going to die," she whispered.

"Brennan—"

"It's not fair!" brennan yelled suddenly. "I had plans. You had plans. We're young, we have lives...why is this happening to us? What did we do that was so wrong?" She began to walk away.

"Where re you going?" Will called after her.

"I don't know. But there's no point staying here anymore."

Instantly she was there, at the place she was shot. It was deserted and she felt compelled to walk forward, to the very spot where she fell.

Will appeared behind her as it all rushed back, everything that had happened that day. "I've always been close to Gabe," she said quietly. "He was born right before I graduated high school, so i was still living with Krista and Wes at the time. Even though I went away to Columbia I came back all the time, and lived there for six months after I graduated until I could afford my own place. They're my family, Will. We're so close and connected...and now we're about to be broken apart, just like our family was when the car crash killed our parents." She looked up at Will. "And I thought, maybe one day, I might have what Wes, Krista, and Gabe have. I don't know what kind of parent I would've been though," she added, smiling wryly.

"Are you kidding? Your first instinct was to protect your nephew, and you took a bullet for him. I think that proves you would be an excellent parent."

"Guess I'll never know, will I?"

Will just looked at her, his blue eyes full of sadness. "You deserve to live," he told her softly.

Brennan touched his cheek. "So do you."

He touched her hand, closing his eyes. "Life doesn't make any sense, does it?"

"Not in our cases," Brennan agreed. Then she paused. "Are you afraid to die?"

"Yes," he admitted. "I'm afraid of the unknown."

"So am I."

Will cleared his throat. "Want to get out of here?"

Brennan nodded, suddenly getting an inspiration. "Let's really get out of here."

"What do you have in mind?" Will asked curiously.

"Remember when we used to talk about going to Paris?" she wanted to know.

"I don't think it'll work, Bren. We've never been there before."

"Who knows what we can do?" Brennan countered. "Maybe if we both just concentrate on it hard enough we'll get there. What do you say? Want to spend a day in Paris with me?" She held out her hand.

He was about to accept it when he suddenly fell forward, writhing in pain. "No!" Brennan screamed, running to him. She could see him start to disappear and grabbed his hand, begging him to fight. Then, before she realized it, they were no longer on the street.

Instead they were sitting on a rooftop, under a glittering night sky. And, unbelievably enough, in the distance was the Eiffel Tower. *We made it,* she thought in amazement. *We made it to Paris.* She looked over to Will, to make sure he was okay.

"We did it, Bren," he said, looking up at the stars. "I kept thinking about Paris though my head felt like it was going to explode...and it worked. We're here." Then he noticed her looking at him strangely. "What is it?"

"You're...different," she said in disbelief.

"Different how?"

"I cn see through you," she told him slowly. "Like you're a ghost or something."

Will looked down at his body and his hands and realized what it meant. "I'm fading," he told her quietly.

"No," she whispered, tears running down her cheeks.

"You knnow, I think I figured it out," he told her after a moment. "Why we found each other like this...it was so we could say good-bye."

"Will-"

"We're both holding on," he told her. "You're still fighting for your family, for your life. I know mine's over. The only reason I'm holding on...is you." He reached for her hand.

Suddenly they were in Will's room, where he was being worked on frantically. "He's hemhorraging!" one nurse yelled.

This time Will didn't writhe in pain. Brennan could tell it was different. "It's time," he told her.

"No-"

He walked over and put his hands on her shoulders, oblivious to the commotion going on around him. "Brennan, I was dead that aneurysm ruptured that night," he told her. "I've only stayed here for you, but that was being selfish because if I let go I can help you."

"How would you dying help me?" Brennan demanded angrily.

"I'm an organ donor."

Brennan understood at once. "No way in hell," she said, backing away. "You're not giving up your life for me."

"You were willing to give up your life for someone you love," he pointed out. "Why can't I do the same?"

Brennan shook her head furiously. "I won't let you do it-"

"My parents love you. They'll go for it."

"No!" Brennan yelled. Then she pulled him to her, kissing him. But unlike with her, his condition didn't change.

He finally pulled away from her. "You have to let me go," he said quietly.

She was crying freely now, shaking her head. "I just found you again and it's been more real to me than anything else-"

"I know. For me too." Then he stepped back. "I love you, Brennan Fox. Take good care of my heart."

"No!" she yelled running toward him. But he disappeared.

Brennan began to scream, yell, and beg in anguish for all the good it did. She saw Will's monitors stop, changing to a steady long beep.

She collapsed to the floor in complete devastation. Then an overwhelmingly bright light encompassed her and she could see Will again. "I'm okay," he called to her. "It's beautiful here, I'm safe and loved, and I'll be watching over you. I'll always be with you, Brennan. Always." Then he and the light vanished.

Brennan laid on the hard hospital floor, curling up into a fetal posistion and squeezing her eyes shut, refusing to ever get up from this spot.

Chapter Eleven

When Brennan finally opened her eyes she was standing on the bridge, feeling completely and utterly alone. Will had moved on, but she was still stuck in limbo.

She remembered coming here before and wanting to jump, though she knew it wouldn't solve anything. Now that Will wasn't here to pull her back, Brennan decided to jump.

Nothing seemed to matter anymore. Will was gone, she was stuck, her family and the Jensens were both in pain...what did it matter if a "spirit" took a header off a bridge? It couldn't make things any worse.

She climbed over the railing, staring at the water far below. *How ironic that Will survived such a crash but was struck down because a blood vessel* erupted in his brain, Brennan thought as she closed her eyes. Stretching her arms open wide she yelled, "I don't care anymore!" up to the heavens, then lept off the bridge.

Brennan could see the water rushing to meet her, though she knew she wouldn't feel it. But then something unexpected happened. The water round her began to shimmer and glow until it was pure white light, engulfing her.

The light slowly separated into the harsh white hospital lights, glaring down at her. Brennan blinked slowly, feeling groggy and disoriented. "What's going on?" she croaked.

It was then she saw she was laying in a hospital bed, hooked up to monitors. She could fuzzily make out several people sitting off to the side, watching her expectantly. The first one was easy to focus on. "Krista?"

Krista lept up from her chair, running to Brennan's side. "You're awake!" she exclaimed, squeezing Brennan's hand. "It really worked." Her tone seemed to sober.

"What worked? What's going on?" Brennan asked weakly. Then she saw Gabe wlk up to her. "Hey little man. Why are you here?"

Krista took a breath. "He's here because of you," she said quietly. "Do you remember?"

"Remember what?"

"A month ago, on Gabe's birthday, you were...shot," Wes spoke up. "You saved our son's life."

"You were in a coma for three weeks," Krista continued, "and your heart was so badly damaged you needed a transplant. You got one and a week later...you're back with us."

Brennan tried to digest it all. "A transplant?" she repeated. Then she could feel the bandages on her chest. "How did I get one so fast?"

Wes and Krista exchanged a look. "Someone passed away a week ago here in the hospital," Krista told her. "He was an organ donor and his family gave the consent when they heard you needed a new heart."

"What's wrong?" Brennan demnded. "What ren't you telling me?" As she said the words they felt incredibly familiar, as if she'd said them recently.

"There's no easy way to say this so maybe we should wait," Krista said, smoothing back Brennan's hair.

"No. I want to know now," Brennan ordered, feeling a sense of urgency. Something was pulling at the back of her mind, like she already knew...

Krista took a deep breath. "The donor was somebody you knew. Someone you knew very well."

Before she could say another word it all came back to Brennan, starting with waking up in her apartment after the shooting, Will finding her on the bridge, all the time they spent together...and what he did for her.

"No," she whispered. "It's not real. No."

"I'm so sorry," Krista said, tears streaming down her face. "It was Will Jensen."

"No!" Brennan cried, struggling to sit up. "I don't want his heart! I want him to have it!" She looked up at her sister desperately. "He should be here too," she whispered, her face streaked with tears.

"He had a brain aneurysm and it erupted," Krista told her softly, though Brennan already knew. "He was braindead, and last week he hemhorraged. The doctor said it was a miracle he held on as long as he did."

Brennan knew why but couldn't say so without everyone thinking she was crazy. She couldn't even appreciate what a relief it was to be seen and heard again, to no longer be stuck between life and death. All she could think about was Will...

"You know much the Jensens love you," Krista continued quietly. "When they heard you needed a new heart...they agreed. They stopped by yesterday."

Brennan continued to cry silently. "It shouldn't have been him," she whispered. "He could've kept fighting. It should've been me—"

"Don't you dare," Krista interrupted. "It shouldn't have been either of you but Will had a brain condition, Bren. If it hadn't happened when it did..."

"...it would've happened later," Brennan finished. "I know, I know." She paused. "It's not that I'm ungrateful," she said quietly. "I just wish—"

"I know," Krista said, kissing her on top of the head and held her close. "I know. But just like you saved Gabe...Will saved you."

But no one could save him, Brennan thought bitterly as she leaned into her sister's shoulder.

He deserved to live too.

***

Brennan was able to attend Will's funeral with the doctor's permission, but was required to have home care for the next few months. When she was finally strong enough, Brennan went out on her own to Hill Park Cememtary.

It was a late, sunny afternoon in mid-July as Brennan opened the black, creaky wrought-iron gate. She started down a row of headstones until she found the right one, then laid the bouquet on his grave.

"Junior prom," she said, kneeling down. "You forgot my corsage so we stopped at a mini-mart and you bought me a purple carnation to match my dress. And then, six months later, you gave me this."

She pulled at the long chain tucked under her shirt that held the silver, ornate class ring Will had given her on their two-year anniversary.

"it was a long time ago," she said, fingering the ring, "and it took me years to get over you, if I ever really did. And what happened between us in April was more real than any other memoryl've ever had.

Some might've called us shadows or spirits but we could think, we could feel, and we could love." She took a breath. "For so long I've kept my heart guarded because all life taught me was if you love someone you'll lose them. But I refuse to keep living that way because you gave me a gift, a second chance. And I promise you I won't waste one second of it. I won't guard your heart; I'll share it. With everyone."

Brennan stood then and unfastened the chain. She removed the ring and kissed it, then carefully laid it on top of the headstone.

William Jacob Jensen

Nov. 15, 1980-Apr. 25, 2008

Beloved Son, Brother, and Friend

When Brennan looked up the sun shone in her face brightly and she had to shield her eyes. As she did she could see a familiar form staring back at her for a long moment. Then Will disappeared into the sunlight.

With one last look at the sun, Brennan turned to go. As she left the cemetary she held her hand lovingly over her new heart.

THE END

Made in the USA
Columbia, SC
08 December 2022

73001150R00061